Can I Play WOLF

Jill Paton Walsh

Illustrated by Jolyne Knox

THE BODLEY HEAD
LONDON

When Gemma's family moved house she had to go to a new school. Gemma liked her old school, but it was too far away from the new house.

On the first day in the new school she felt very shy. And the new school was very confusing for her, because the children and the teachers kept doing things wrong.

In Gemma's old school the windows were always kept shut, in case of draughts. Miss Simpson didn't like draughts.

In the new school the teacher was a very large lady wearing a lovely pink track suit, and she made the children open all the windows. She said fresh air would blow away the cobwebs.

In Gemma's old school there was a very important rule about not helping with another child's work. But in the new school whenever someone got stuck at the reading book, the pink lady said 'can anyone help?', and lots of children crowded round, and did the reading for the child who was stuck.

Gemma couldn't do the sums in the number book the pink lady gave her, and a big boy called Robert came and did them for her. In Gemma's old school that would have been called cheating, but in the new school they just called it helping.

In Gemma's old school you had to ask if you wanted to go to the toilet. In the new school you just got up and found your way there and back. Because Gemma was new, the pink lady sent a girl called Barbara with her to show her the way.

Gemma's old school had a fish tank in the corner of the classroom with two fish, called Moby Dick and Jaws, swimming in it. Miss Simpson said it wasn't hygienic to keep an animal indoors, but she would make an exception for fish. But the new school had an indoor rabbit called Starsky, who crunched carrot while the pink lady was telling things to the class. Starsky did smell a little bit, but only of carrot and warm straw.

In Gemma's old school they never did gym straight after break. Miss Simpson said it would be bad for them to jump around when they were full of milk and biscuits. But the pink lady hadn't thought of that; she made them all jump over benches and swing on ropes like monkeys, as soon as they had finished eating and drinking.

Gemma thought everyone would be sick, but they weren't. Gemma wasn't sick either, but she *was* feeling very funny. She didn't like the way everything was being done wrong. She almost didn't like the pink lady. But the worst time for her was the beginning of playtime. All the children ran out into the playground, and began to run and shout, and Gemma was all by herself, watching them.

A girl called Alice came up to Gemma. 'Don't you want to play?' she asked.

'Don't know,' said Gemma, feeling so shy it made her cheeks hot.

'Of course you do,' said Alice. 'Come on, let's ask Robert.' Alice took Gemma's hand, and pulled her across the playground.

Robert was in charge of the game. Alice and Gemma went up to him.

'Well, go on, Gemma!' said Alice. 'Ask him!'

'Can I play?' Gemma asked. Her voice came out very soft.

'Yes,' he said. 'We're playing Wolf.'

'I don't know how to play that,' said Gemma.

'It's easy,' said Robert. 'Listen, and say what all the others say. Look and do the same as all the others do.'

So Gemma looked, and listened.

All the children stood in a ring, and Robert counted round them. Each time he said a word in his rhyme, he touched someone in the ring. This is what he said:

'Eenie, meenie, macka racka,
Rare, rare, Dominacker,
Chocka blocka lolly poppa
Im, pim, pom, PUSH!'

The girl he was pointing to when he got as far as PUSH! stepped out of the ring. Then he counted round again, saying it again, and someone else stepped out. The third time he did it, he counted out Gemma. He went on until there was only one person left, and that was Alice.

'Alice, you're the Wolf this time,' said Robert.

'Now let's choose the Shepherd,' said Alice. She went along the line of waiting children, counting each one. This is what she said:

'Dip, dip, dip,
My blue ship,
Sailing on the water,
Like a cup and saucer,
You – are – IT!'

When she got to the end she was pointing at a boy called Gary.

'Gary is the Shepherd!' everyone said.

Then the game began. First Gary, being Shepherd, went to one end of the playground all by himself. The children who were sheep stayed close together at the other end. Alice the Wolf went and crouched down out of sight behind the caretaker's skip, about half way.

Then Gary the Shepherd called out, 'Sheep, sheep, come home!'

Everyone answered, 'We can't!' Everyone except for Gemma, that is, she didn't know the words yet.

'Why not?' called Gary.

'We're afraid!' everyone answered.

'What of?' called Gary

'The *Wolf*!' shouted the children. Gemma felt shivery at the back of her neck, even though she knew the Wolf was only Alice, pretending.

But Gary the Shepherd
called back,

*'The Wolf has gone to
Devonshire,
And won't be back for seven
year!
Sheep, sheep, come home!'*

Then everybody ran, as hard as they could, all running towards the Shepherd's end of the playground, and as they rushed past her, Alice ran out and grabbed a little boy and held on to him.

'What happens now?' asked Gemma, a little out of breath from running fast.

'Now there are two wolves to catch us, and we do it again,' Robert told her.

Gary the Shepherd went to the other end of the playground, and called them again, 'Sheep, sheep, come home!

'We can't!' everyone shouted.

'Why not?' called Gary,

'We're afraid!' called the sheep – just the same as before. This time Gemma shouted too, as loud as anyone.

'What of?'

'The *Wolf*!'

Gary chanted:

'The Wolf has gone to Devonshire,
And won't be back for seven year!'
Sheep, sheep, come home!'

Everybody ran again, and Lucy got caught, so then there were three wolves. The Shepherd changed ends, and they did it all again. It felt lovely and scary being chased by wolves, even though Gemma knew the wolves were only children pretending.

Everyone ran as hard as they could go, and screamed when a wolf-child got near. Gemma got caught about the seventh time. She ran as hard as she could, but Lucy ran faster, and grabbed hold of Gemma's skirt. So Gemma changed from being a sheep to a wolf.

She was a bit cross at first, but it was just as much fun being a wolf and trying to catch a sheep as it was being a sheep trying not to be caught by a wolf. When you were a wolf you made growly noises, and ran and pounced at the poor frightened sheep. Gemma was good at the snarling noises.

As the game went on there were more and more wolves, and the sheep got caught more and more quickly, until there was only one sheep left, and that was a little boy called Lawrence, who could run very fast, and go zigzag instead of straight.

And before they could start again, the bell rang for the end of break.

'Is Lawrence the winner?' Gemma asked Robert.

'It isn't a game with winners and losers,' Robert told her. 'It's just what we play.'

'You're a winner, Gemma,' said Alice. 'We like everyone who joins in.'

Gemma felt very pleased. She decided that she liked the pink lady, and she liked the rabbity smell in the classroom. 'Can we get Starsky out to play, Mrs Bell?' Robert asked the pink lady.

'Not this afternoon, Robert,' the pink lady said, 'we still have number work to do.'

And Gemma bravely spoke up. 'Oh, please,' she said, 'because I've never played with a rabbit before in my whole life!'

'Oh, all right then,' said Mrs. Bell, smiling at Gemma. 'We'll let Starsky out as a special first day treat for Gemma. Close the windows before you open the hutch door, children...'

'Because he might jump right through the window, and get out into the playground,' Gary said, 'and it's dangerous for him because...'

'Because the playground is full of wolves!' said Gemma, and everybody laughed.

Later, when Gemma was telling her mother all about her first day at school, she told her how to play Wolf.

'That's funny,' said Gemma's mother. 'I used to play Wolf when I was a little girl. But our Wolf didn't go to Devonshire, he went to Lancashire.'

'That wouldn't be as good,' said Gemma. 'Lancashire doesn't rhyme with "seven year" properly.'

'Ah,' said mother. 'But our Wolf didn't go for seven year, he went to buy a penny handkershire!'

'The Wolf has gone to Lancashire, to buy a penny handkershire,' said Gemma, trying what it sounded like. 'I wonder which is right?'

'They're both right,' said mother. 'There isn't always a right and wrong to things.'

'There isn't always a winner and a loser, you know,' said Gemma. 'Sometimes it's just what we play.'

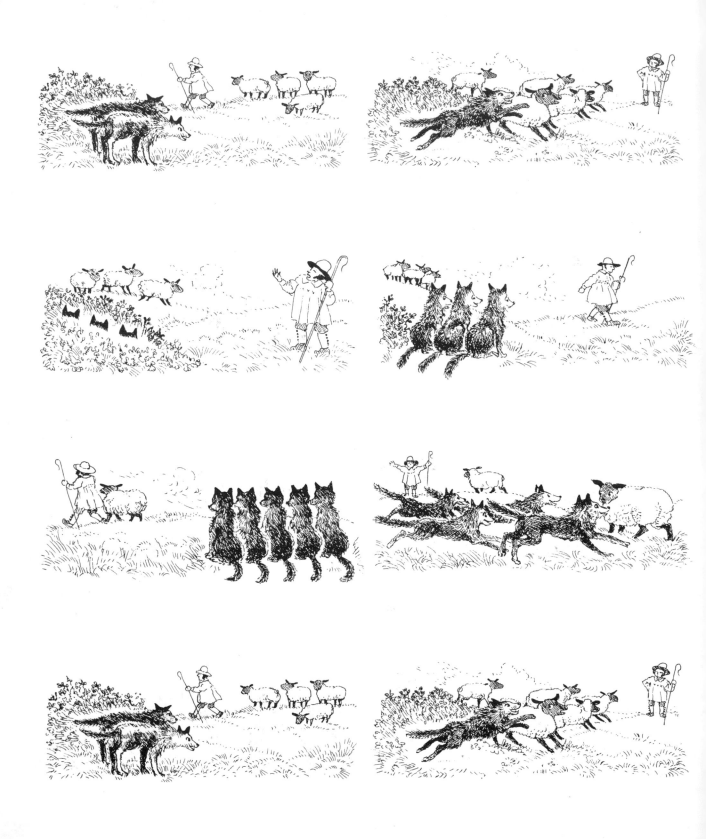